Chapter 1

Freak dog

It all started with three promises – one from Max and two from his sister Amy.

Promise 1

Max upset Amy by filming her all the time.

"Do something funny," he told her. "Then I can put it on the Internet and we'll be famous."

Mum made Max stop filming Amy.

"If she doesn't want you to do it, don't do it," she said.

"OK," he said. "I promise!"

Promise 2

Amy asked her parents for a dog.

"I'll look after it," she promised.

"Will you walk it in the rain?" asked Dad.

"Yes," Amy replied.

"Will you pick up its poo in a bag?" he asked.

"Er…yes," Amy nodded.

Amy's mum and dad liked the idea of a dog. They just wanted Amy to understand how much work it was. In the end they agreed.

"OK," said Mum. "But we need to find a dog from a good home."

Amy already had a website on her phone.

"This dog is cute," she said. "His name is Tag."

Max looked at the photo. "Wow!" he grinned. "Freak dog! He's got wonky eyes!"

When they went to meet Tag he did look pretty funny. One of his eyes was a different colour. His fur stuck up too. It looked like there was hair wax in it.

"That makes him cool," said Amy. "Tag is coming home with us."

Promise 3

Max started filming Tag on his phone.

"This dog is crazy-looking," he told Amy. "He's going to be an Internet star!"

"If you put Tag on the Internet I will throw your phone in the toilet!" Amy cried. "That is a promise!"

Chapter 2

No, Tag!

The first time Amy took Tag to the park they walked past a boy eating crisps. Before she could stop Tag, he stuck his nose in the crisp bag.

"Hey!" shouted the angry boy. "That dog drooled on my cheese and onion crisps."

Amy had to go and buy him another packet.

Worse was to come the next day. Tag ran over to a woman having her packed lunch.

"Stop, Tag!" Amy cried, but he took no notice. He tried to snuffle his way into the woman's lunch box.

"Ever heard of dog training?" the woman snapped crossly.

Amy told her Dad what had happened.

"He isn't a bad dog," said Dad. "He's just got to get used to your voice."

Dad didn't feel the same after Tag chewed one of his trainers.

"That dog needs to learn some rules," he grumbled.

"Way to go, freak dog!" said Max when he heard what Tag did. "Please let me film him."

"No way!" snapped Amy. "Remember what I said about your phone in the toilet."

Amy was glad that Max wasn't with her when she took Tag to dog training class.

"What a sweet dog," said the teacher.

She didn't feel the same when Tag stuck his nose in her bag and pulled out some mints.

"That dog has no manners," she muttered.

Amy's friend Milly thought it was a great idea to put Tag on the Internet. That was before she met him.

"If he's cute he will get loads of likes," she said on the phone.

When she came round and saw Tag she wasn't quite so sure.

"He's a bit weird-looking," she said. "What he needs is a makeover."

Chapter 3

Tag does WHAT?

Max came in to see what the girls were doing.

"I HAVE to film this!" he cried, as Milly began to brush Tag's fur.

"No!" Amy snapped.

"I won't put it on the Internet," Max replied.

"It is just for us to look at," he insisted. "Then I'll delete it."

"OK. Just this once," Amy replied.

Milly began to tie silly ribbons on Tag's fur.

"He looks REALLY crazy now," Max giggled.

"Don't put on any more," said Amy.

"Just ONE more," Milly begged. "Please! He looks so cute!"

"Woof," barked Tag, lifting his paw.

"Yes, that's right. One," laughed Milly.

"Woof," Tag barked again and lifted his paw.

Max crouched down in front of Tag.

"Two," he said.

"Woof, woof," Tag barked, then he lifted his paw twice.

"Three," Max said.

"Woof, woof, woof," Tag barked and lifted his paw three times.

"The dog is a genius!" Max cried.

It turned out that Tag could count up to five.

"Where did he come from?" Milly asked.

"The Dog Rescue Centre," Amy replied.
"He was found in the park."

"Somebody must have loved Tag once," said
Milly. "They trained him to count. But why?"

"To make him a star!" cried Max.

Amy and Milly went to find Tag a dog treat. When they came back Max was looking guilty.

"Don't get mad, Amy," he said. "You'll thank me in the end."

"What do you mean?" asked Amy, puzzled.

"He's posted some film of Tag counting," said Milly, looking at her phone.

"No!" cried Amy. "I'm going to drown your phone, Max!"

"Only a few friends are going to see the film," insisted Max. "Then I'll delete it."

But Max was wrong. By the next day Tag's film had one thousand likes, and the number was going up.

Tag had gone viral.

Chapter 4

The superstar with a wet nose

Fans began writing comments under Tag's Internet film.

Weird dog. He's great.

Clever dude.

Hey, crazy eyes. Keep counting!

Meanwhile, Amy's schoolfriends had begun sending her messages.

Is that your dog? He's so cool!

Can your dog do my homework?

Someone told a local radio reporter and he turned up at the front door.

"Your dog is trending online," said the reporter. "Can he really count?"

Before Amy could stop him, Tag ran up to the reporter. The man bent down, grinning.

"Hey, cute guy. Can you count to three?" he asked.

"Woof, woof, woof," barked Tag.

"I don't want any fuss," cried Amy.

She felt knotted up inside. Someone had trained Tag to count. If they had lost him by mistake they would hear about him on the radio or see him online. They would want him back!

At that moment Dad came in from the garden.

"How do you feel about having a genius dog?" the reporter asked him.

"What?" Dad replied.

Then Mum walked in.

"A local TV film crew just phoned up," she said. "They are on their way round."

"What?" said Dad.

Then Max ran in.

"Tag has two thousand likes," he cried.

"WHAT?" Dad cried. "Can somebody please tell me what is going on?"

Amy's eyes filled with tears, as her phone pinged with more texts.

"Go away everyone!" she cried. If this went on, she was going to lose Tag. She was going to have to give him back to his real owner.

The doorbell rang again. This time it was a man with a coat under his arm.

"I've come to get my dog," he said.

Chapter 5

A liar at the door

Everybody stood staring at the man.

"I've come to get my dog," he repeated. "It's mine. I lost it. Come here, Tag. Good boy, Tag."

Tag didn't move.

"Wait a minute," said Dad. "How do we know Tag is your dog?"

"I've cleared things with the Dog Rescue Centre," the man replied.

"What's your name?" the radio reporter asked.

The man did not reply. Amy knew instantly that he was a liar. She went to pick up Tag, but the man was quicker. He snatched Tag up and bundled him in his coat.

"No!" Amy shouted, but the man turned and ran. They chased after him but they were too late. He jumped in the back of a car that roared off up the road.

"I'll ring the police right now," Dad cried. "We'll get Tag back somehow."

"I'll post online. Everyone will want to help find him," added Max.

"It's all your fault!" Amy shouted at him. "You told everyone about him. Now he's gone!"

"I'm sorry. I'll help you find him," said Max. "I promise I will."

Just then the film crew arrived from the local TV station.

"We've come to film the cute counting dog," they explained.

34

"He's been stolen," Max told them. "But I can help. I can send you a film of Tag. Will you put it on TV and ask everyone to help find him?"

The film was shown on the news that night.

"The thieves who stole Tag may want to sell him to make money," said the TV presenter. That made Amy feel really angry.

"I promised to look after Tag and I will," she insisted. "I won't give up until I find him again!"

Chapter 6

Have you seen Tag?

Friends began to send out messages online, along with Tag's picture. Strangers shared his picture online, too. Amy and Milly even made lots of posters to put around town.

But after two or three weeks nothing had happened. People stopped talking about it. Only Amy, Milly and Max refused to give up.

One day Amy and Milly saw the radio reporter in the supermarket.

"I guess Tag is still missing," he said. Amy blinked back tears.

"Can you remember anything about the thief?" she asked. "We don't have a single clue."

"Well, I think his car was brown," said the reporter. "I'm not sure, though."

"Ok, thanks," said Amy, but her heart sank. The clue was no help. Perhaps the search for Tag really was over.

When they got home they found Max sitting in the kitchen.

"Someone left a parcel on the doorstep for you," he said.

The parcel was wrapped in brown paper and had small neat writing on it. It said 'For Amy'.

Amy was amazed when she opened it. Inside there was a dog bowl with the name TAG on it.

"Is this a sick joke?" Milly frowned.

"I don't think so," said Amy. "There's a packet of cheese and onion crisps and some mints in here, too. They're Tag's favourites!"

Max looked at a letter that had been tucked into the parcel.

"Someone called Fred wrote this," he said. "He says he trained Tag and he wants us to go and see him. He lives in an old people's home near the park."

"Let's go right now!" Amy cried. "We have to know if Fred is for real."

Chapter 7

Tag's big secret

They found Fred in an old people's home, just a couple of streets away.

"I'm glad you came to see me," he smiled. "It shows how much you care about Tag. I'm sorry I couldn't help sooner. I've been ill, you see.

Then yesterday I heard somebody talking about a counting dog who went missing. I knew it had to be Tag, so I found out more. Now I've got something to show you."

Fred had some old photos of two dogs.
They were rolling big balls along and waving
their paws at the camera.

"These dogs were called Billy and May," said
Fred. "My dad trained them to appear on stage.
They were called The Genius Dogs."

"They look just like Tag," smiled Milly.

"Tag is from a long line of their puppies," nodded Fred. "I trained him to count — just for old time's sake. I could never stop him stealing crisps or mints, though!"

"How did you lose him?" asked Max.

"A man saw us counting in the park one day," said Fred. "He wanted to buy Tag, but I said no. We went home and a few minutes later I found the back door open. Tag was missing."

"The man followed you home and stole him!" Amy gasped.

"That's right," Fred nodded. "I asked around and found out he lived at 5 Rose Street."

"I called by and a woman opened the door," Fred went on. "She told me to go away. She said they didn't have a dog. I knew she was lying, but then I fell ill. I had to go to hospital and now I'm here. Tag must have escaped from Rose Street."

"And now he's back there," cried Amy. "I'm sure of it!"

Chapter 8

Run!

"Let me ring your parents," suggested Fred. "It's best to let them sort this out. People who steal dogs aren't good people. You should stay away from them."

The children knew Fred was talking sense but they wanted to help. When they left the old people's home they headed for Rose Street.

"Let's just go and see the house," said Amy. "We won't knock or anything."

The others agreed. They would just look…

Number 5 was quiet. Nobody was around outside. There was an alleyway along the side of the house. From there they could see over the garden fence.

"There's a dog in the back room. I can see it through the glass door," said Amy. "I'm going to take a closer look."

51

Quick as a flash, she climbed over the fence and ran over. It was Tag! His fur looked darker. They had used dye to change its colour, but they couldn't change his funny eyes.

Amy put her fingers to the door. She pushed gently and it slid open.

"Woof!" barked Tag, jumping into her arms.

"Some kid is taking the dog!" shouted a woman.
Then someone pushed past her into the room.
It was the man who had stolen Tag. His face was
screwed up with anger.

"Run!" yelled Max at the top of his voice.

For once Amy listened to her brother.

Chapter 9

Get him!

The man shot after Amy, but she made it into the alleyway. She held tightly onto Tag but it was hard to run fast and carry the little dog too.

"Follow me!" cried Max. They ducked into another alleyway, then another. The man chased them, his shoes pounding on the path as he ran.

Amy stumbled, but Milly grabbed her arm to steady her.

"Come on!" gasped Milly. "He's catching up!"

They ran towards the park, but the woman from Rose Street had got there first.

"Quick! Hide in the bushes," hissed Max.

From their hiding place they saw the man arrive.

"That dog has got to be here somewhere," he said to the woman. "Let's look around."

Amy, Max and Milly froze, trying not to breathe.
Then Amy saw a person on a bench nearby.
It was the boy who ate cheese and onion crisps!
He was taking a packet out of his pocket...

"No!" cried Amy, but it was too late. Tag leapt
from her arms, towards the beloved crisps.

"Look!" shouted the man. "There's the dog!"

His wife dived for Tag, grabbed him and ran. In a moment they were gone.

"I can't believe it!" groaned Amy. "I've made things worse."

Nobody said it out loud, but they were all very worried. The thieves might get rid of Tag now to save trouble.

They trudged out of the park, not knowing what to do. But when they reached the end of Rose Street they stopped and stared. There was Dad with Fred, standing next to a police car.

"Dad? What's going on?" Amy cried.

Chapter 9

Rescue

"Fred phoned me an hour ago," Dad explained.
"I picked him up and we came right over.
I called the police, too. When we got here we
saw two people running up the road with Tag.
They're inside talking to the police now."

Soon a policewoman came out carrying Tag.

"They dyed his fur, but we know it's him," she smiled. "He counts!"

Fred gave Tag a hug, then handed him to Amy.

"This little fella can't live with me anymore,"
he told her. "But I'd be happy if I knew he was
living with you."

Amy couldn't stop smiling.

The children began taking Tag to visit Fred. Max even started to teach Fred to use the Internet. Then one day Max made a surprise announcement.

"We've put Tag on the Internet again," he said.

"No way!" Amy cried.

"Don't explode," Max grinned. "Nobody will recognize him." He showed her his screen.

"I've made a cartoon dog that looks like Tag," he said. "He moves his paws to a beat. I was going to call him DJ Freak. What do you think?"

"How about DJ Genius?" laughed Amy. "What do you reckon, Tag? How many points will you give Max for his cartoon?"

She whispered in Tag's ear.

"Woof," said Tag, five times over.